America's First
Commercial Airfield

America's First Commercial Airfield

and Lyman Gilmore Junior

R.A. LAND

ILLUSTRATED BY CHRIS MARINAN AND BILL BRUCE

To order additional copies of this book, contact:
Xlibris Corporation
1-888-795-4274
www.Xlibris.com
Orders@Xlibris.com
30239

CONTENTS

This book is dedicated to the
people who believed
in Lyman Gilmore Jr.

The Airship now goes round and round
The bands begin to play
Man is about to spread his wings
And sail the Milky Way.
  —Prospectus of the Gilmore Airship Company

Introduction

The aviation industry has made insurmountable progress in the past century. Rockets thrust outside the atmosphere orbit the earth or land on distant planets. Passenger planes carry us from place to place and are a part of our everyday lives. We are on the frontier of new horizons in space exploration and commercial space travel.

However, about one hundred years ago, man was experimenting with the most primitive forms of flight. Single- and two-engine airplanes that were heavier than air were being invented by a few clever and courageous men. Among them were the Wright brothers. They are still widely known for their contribution of the first powered heavier-than-air plane to lift off the ground.

There were others not so well known yet still contributors to the progress of aviation. One of these men was Lyman Gilmore Jr. Lyman's talent as an inventor and engineer led him to create the first flying field west of the Mississippi River. As years progressed, this field would be recognized as the first commercial airfield in the United States. The airfield contained formal elements of modern airports we use today. Located in the Sierra Nevada foothills of California, the tiny field of fifty acres stood for many years until 1968 when a junior high school was built.

Lyman Gilmore Jr. was born in the late nineteenth century. He became known in the area he worked and lived as the "Eagle of the Sierras." A few of the inventions and plane innovations that affect how we live today were created in his workshops. Unfortunately, newspaper stories written during the years of his experiences with aviation as well as modern accounts of those activities often have conflicting dates and information. There are differing opinions about when Mr. Gilmore was born and where his birthplace was. Questions still exist about when his first planes were built, when he flew them, and whether he invented the world's first powered glider. An ongoing debate has survived for many years about whether Lyman Gilmore Jr. flew a powered heavier-than-air plane before the Wright brothers. The popular exaggeration of tales told by the early miners may have also colored the truth about his life. As a result, in stories retold about him, facts are woven with folklore.

The following story captures some of the events of this brilliant yet mysterious man's lifetime. These include the building of Mr. Gilmore's airfield and his two famous monoplanes, the creation of his stock company, and his epochal glider flight in 1902. Changes in transportation occurring throughout the period are also mentioned.

I hope you will enjoy this biography based on a true story and an interesting piece of history's past.

Chapter One

The Day and Age of
Lyman Gilmore Jr.'s Ancestors

In the sixteenth century, ships from England carried immigrants to America. Among these new settlers were Lyman Gilmore Jr.'s ancestors. They settled along the East Coast of North America living in New England.

* * *

Early in the 1800s and farther down the eastern coastline was New York City, a thriving, bustling settlement and seaport. Buildings of brownstone, scrap metal, or wood sat on cobblestone or dirt streets. Children selling fruit, hot corn, or pie stood on street corners. Horse-drawn wagons and carriages taking travellers away to another settlement or just down the road apiece hobbled on wooden wheels. People of many different nations lived here. Some worked on docks or wharves. On the bay were big ships sailing into view. Other ships, filled with the curious, left the port city for many destinations.

Lyman Gilmore Jr.'s grandfather was among those who set sail from New York to prospect around the world. First, Grandfather Gilmore sailed around the Cape Horn of South America. Travelling this route was a difficult thing to do. Cape Horn was a strait at the southern tip of South America that connected the South Atlantic and South Pacific oceans. Passage around the horn was treacherous. Heavy ocean storms and icebergs made the strait almost impossible to pass through. The courageous Gilmore reached Peru and mined there before leaving for Australia.

The tale of an old Spanish legend promising that the Stanislaus River in California was flowing over sands of gold beckoned him to head for San Francisco, California. He came, but his stay wasn't long, for he found little gold. The adventurer sailed once again to Peru.

Suddenly a lot of gold had been discovered in California. The gold strike was on! This was now where magic finds of the ore would be made. Grandfather Gilmore boarded another ship. It is probable that he was aboard one of the few mail steamers that rounded the cape, stopping in Peru to take up anxious miners who anticipated making fortunes in California. He sailed to California finally settling in the goldfields of Calaveras County in 1852.

More and more settlers began a movement to lure people from everywhere to go west in hopes of finding golden treasures. Grandfather Gilmore's son Lyman and Sarah Augusta Gray were living on the eastern seaboard in Maine with their many relatives and respective families at the time. They would join others entrapped by gold fever and yearning for land. The two would eventually live in one gold mining area in Calaveras County in California. Following Grandfather Gilmore's footsteps, they would settle in the Mokelumne Hill area to make their new home in the west.

Mokelumne Hill itself was a settlement in the southern Sierra Nevada. It became one of the first gold camps in mining country. Mining began along the Mokelumne River in 1848. Tents were soon set up, and a camp was established. This settlement was known as a wild one and for its many fires.

Some say that Lyman came to this area in California sometime between 1852 and 1860. Sarah would come later. During some of the years in the decade before 1860, Lyman would mine. He left the area at times travelling to the Sierra Nevada to search for gold at a place called Red Dog.

In the same decade, more women were coming to Mokelumne Hill, many wanting a place where they could worship. A congregational church was built in the settlement as a result of charitable donations from the miners.

Newcomers to the area saw other changes. Stores, once mere tents and wooden shacks, were now being replaced by stone and adobe buildings. Camps here were joining other settlements in the progress of the west as houses, churches, bakeries, stores, and banks began to evolve, catering to citizens and immigrants alike.

In 1854, changes in transportation started taking place. Until now, mail, supplies, even people had been transported by horses, oxen, horse-

and mule-driven wagons, boats, and vessels sailing from harbor to harbor. Now horse-drawn carriages began carrying mail and supplies inland and unloading goods at the harbors. The progress continued as the first stages of the Transcontinental Railroad began in 1863. Trains would begin to replace slower modes of transporting goods and people.

The Civil War raged during the years of 1861 through 1865. Two years after the war was over, Lyman and Sarah were married in Penobscot, Maine. They would begin to start their family in the Mokelumne Hill area of California. A housekeeper, Sarah Gilmore would bear five children in Rich Gulch, a mining community that was in the same county as Mokelumne Hill.

Lillian Gertrude, Sarah's first child, was born in 1867. A sister, Eunice, followed in 1869. One year later, a boy, Charles Hartson, came into the world. Sarah's son Samuel's birth occurred in October of 1872. The last child, born to the pioneer woman in California, was Elmer in 1875.

Like so many newcomers to the west, the Gilmores left in the exodus from the gold vein of California. They uprooted the family and rode north to settlements in the northwest called the Washington Territory.

Chapter Two

Lyman Junior's Boyhood

The Gilmores and their five children arrived in Thurston County of the Washington Territory near a place called Olympia. Families in towns and cities now forming throughout the west were summoned to mining and farming as ways at making a living. The Gilmores settled into farm life and continued to have children. The sixth of their eleven offspring was named Lyman Wiswell Gilmore. The dark haired baby with blue eyes was born on June 11, 1876, in Beaver Creek, although some say he was born in another place called Sightly. To tell him apart from his father, the boy would be called Lyman Junior.

Sisters Lillian, Eunice, and a brother Charles were already in school. Lyman had a baby brother in August of 1878 when Sarah gave birth to John Wallace. A girl, Olive Maria, was born two years later. The last child to be born in Beaver Creek was Fredrick Blaine in 1883.

Now during this time, homesteads or farms were scattered apart; and one farm may be a half mile or as many as twenty miles away from a neighboring farm.

Here, the youngster, Lyman Junior, spent his childhood with unusual interests. He loved to read and make machine-driven toys. However, his favorite thing to do was to look at things that would glide in the sky. Hours of walking and observing gliding birds like the buzzard, condor, eagle, and swan would take up much of his time. This, along with his schooltime passion for drawing and creating diagrams, led him to create objects resembling birds. Entranced by his observations, the young boy would come home and tell his mother what he saw. Many times he would ramble on about his ideas while they did the dishes together. Thus, his mother nicknamed him "Mr. Stretchit."

Lyman Junior's brothers and sisters didn't care for this daydreaming of sorts. As young children are, they preferred the art of playing hoops and marbles or jackstraws after their chores were done. The young thinker, on the other hand, didn't play as much. He was just too preoccupied with watching feathered creatures travelling through air. When little Lyman was disregarded by others, as he sometimes was, his mother and grandmother were supportive and would provide comfort by reading to him.

It has been said that some of Lyman Junior's relatives were famous, one of which was an army surgeon. Also, his grandfather was a general. Some of Lyman's other relatives at the time were of mechanical nature. This may have had something to do with the boy's fascination with machines. He also had a desire to use and apply the knowledge of science for practical purposes.

Further south, Cowlitz County lent itself to mining and farming. The Columbia River ran alongside the county line. The river provided water for farming, and gold was prospected along its waters. Lumbering was also a way to survive. So by oxen, the Gilmores came to settle once again, this time to Castle Rock. In 1885, Lyman Junior's brother Edwin Herman Grant was born near here in a place called Sightly.

Sometime after his eleventh birthday, so some say, Lyman Junior constructed his first airplane model from wood. A pole atop the family woodshed kept the plane in place for a long while.

About two years later, Sarah Gilmore would give birth to her last child, Harrison Gray, who was born in July of 1889.

By this time, young Lyman Junior's interest in flight started to consume him. His love of machines and birds flying continued. In high school, he read a poem in a book one day, "When man has robbed from the eagle his eagle secret, then man shall be able to soar through the air unconcerned." These were words of inspiration to him.

During his fourteenth year, Lyman and some friends of his changed an old building at a nearby creek into a workshop. They helped make the creek higher and stronger by building a kind of paddle wheel that may have helped generate electricity for the shop. Some projects that Lyman Junior worked on there were the building of a steam-powered boat and a ship five feet in length. The ship had a distinct arrangement of masts, rigging, and sails.

Lyman Junior and his father measured the weight of a swan one day and found that the wing of the bird gave four pounds of lifting power to the foot. This was one of the first experiments that led to some of the young man's later discoveries regarding powered flight.

Later, the boy completed high school. His mother raise money to help him get some formal schooling to study the basics of mechanical engineering and drafting. He was schooled at Pullman Agricultural College in Washington. In his spare time, young Junior spent times at the ocean watching how the seabirds moved, particularly seagulls.

Now the young inventor, a bright and clever lad, started to experiment with flight during his summer vacation in 1891. It was his belief that man should be able to fly through the sky as easily as the birds. To promote this idea, he attached flapping wings to a bicycle. He used pedals connected to a driveshaft instead of a chair. Lyman made the wings go up and down using his arms and hands. This, in turn, made the propeller of the makeshift contraption go around as he went down a hill and into the wind. Down, down the hill he went to see if he could lift it off the ground. It did lift a little, with some saying it stayed in the air for several hundred feet before landing. Oh, what a feeling it must have been to conquer Mother Nature!

One question that seemed to stump the young man was how to make a plane's wings flap without carrying too much weight in the motors. He decided, at least for now, to concentrate on building gliders. Gliders didn't require motors to make them move. Lyman Junior then built his first glider. That same year, he also built a ten-foot sailplane model.

The boy continued, determined to pursue his dream. He soon managed to create a set of drawings of a glider. These sketches were based on the idea of what made the giant condor fly. Two years later, he would be ready to build a glider based on these drawings. As time went on, Lyman Junior's father, Lyman Senior, began investing in flying materials from money he had originally saved to further his son's education. Yet after seeing the teenager's foibles, he started to shrug any hopes for the boy's success. Father Gilmore disapproved of young Lyman's desire to create flying contraptions and called his son's pastime "tomfoolery." He told the boy that he should forget about tinkering with flying a plane by mechanical means and go to a nearby balloon farm to learn to fly. In those days, men flew into the sky using air balloons.

Lyman Junior's brothers and sisters as well wondered why their brother was spending more time with his flying interests than helping out with chores on the farm.

Despite his families' concerns, Lyman Junior was beset by a unique determination to continue his projects. Soon after, in 1894 he left for California.

Chapter Three

Lyman Junior's First Experiments

Now the town of Redding was the county seat of Shasta County and was a respected city. The Sacramento River ran through this area. The California and Oregon railroads met here for many years. The nearby town of Red Bluff sat on a plateau. Ferries were common here and a necessary means of carrying goods and mail to the area. Farms and ranches, spread out by distance, dotted the countryside. Views of low-lying bald hills could be seen. Jackrabbits scampered across the meadowland.

Lyman Junior arrived here with a passion for gliders, and a promise to continue. They say he lived in the area on John Gilmore's sheep ranch with his older brother Samuel. The boy's parents and some of his brothers and sisters had lived about two hundred miles from here in Rich Gulch some twenty years earlier. But for Lyman, who saw and studied the likes of the lands up north, this new California land full of fields and hills he hoped would be able to fulfill his flying dreams.

Now other men who lived in California had already been experimenting with flying planes or airships as they were called then. An Englishman named Frederick Marriot had already designed and built the avitor. This balloonlike contraption was the first type of plane to fly in the United States. It didn't even look like the planes we see today.

They say that when Lyman Junior wasn't milking cows or making hay, he was busy with his flying experiments. He began by building a canvas-covered glider. He used the design patterned after the giant condor that he had created two years earlier. The plane was flown again and again until Lyman could get it to fly steady.

According to legend, the boy spent a lot of time on the ranch continuing his flight experiments in unusual ways. One story that has been passed down through the years is that one day, without any of the ranch owner's knowledge, Lyman Junior built a wooden model glider with a ten-foot wingspan. He then plucked feathers from some of the farm's turkeys and attached them to the frame of the craft to see if this would help it fly. Unconventional as he was, he couldn't resist using anything he could think of to make it lift up. Maybe turkey feathers would do it.

Now the development of the railroad was slowly replacing the horse-drawn stages, steamers, and Pony Express for transporting mail and some forms of freight by 1894. Post offices had been established in many cities around the country by this time. Even so, the American railway strike halted mail delivery in 1894. All trains operating between Chicago and San Francisco were stopped. Freight, cattle, and mail needed to be moved. The influential people of the railroads became very angry and tried to destroy many trains. President Grover Cleveland ordered troops of federal soldiers to stop the fury.

Young Lyman, like everyone in the West, was concerned about the event. He tried to make a plane that would carry mail. He built a primitive rigid glider with muslin-covered wings. He coated the wings with glue and rosin after allowing a pastelike mixture to dry. The wings spanned about eighteen feet. It had some features of a monoplane.

He then found a suitable place where he could take his aircraft.

The experiment was done in a field. Lyman would run along the ground using his feet as takeoff and landing gear. This worked a few times as the craft lifted, but it became somewhat uncontrollable.

Later, he found a better way to get it up. According to legend, the glider was drawn by a horse who trotted to the top of a hill, then did the same down the hill with the contraption attached. Suddenly, a towrope fastening the horse to the glider tightened as the craft lifted up to eighteen feet in the air and flew for about five hundred feet. One man who was helping Lyman Junior by riding on the horse became excited by all this. He proceeded to yell loudly and then threw his hat into the air. As a result, the horse became startled, jerked the rope, and the change in air pressure of the great glider sailing above caused it to dive toward the ground. The horse, now spooked more than ever, scurried to a barn one mile away.

Like his father, who had mined in California some twenty years earlier, Lyman Junior also mined during his stay at the ranch. His mining activities took him within Shasta County and to nearby Trinity County.

As time went on, the people on the ranch didn't share Lyman's enthusiasm for creating "flying machines." So in 1895, after reaction from the disgruntled ranchers and requests from his relatives, legend says the young fellow rode a bicycle. He headed toward the western slope of the northern hills of the Sierra Nevada.

Here Lyman Junior spent some time in a place called Dutch Flat. This area was about eleven miles up the way from the town of Colfax and on the northeast side. It was higher up in the mountains. They say that he lived with his brother Charles and his youngest brother Harrison for about a year and that they worked on building a wooden model airplane spanning three feet. Dutch Flat, like other foothill settlements, was protected by tall incensed cedars with their flat sprays as well as other evergreens. It has been said that here, as a young man, Lyman Junior used to sit on the mountain slopes and watch the landing and taking off of eagles.

Later the youth ended up living between Colfax and Iowa Hill. The area was primitive and undeveloped. A winding wagon road used for stagecoaches began in Colfax and wound down toward the American River. The road continued on the other side of the river looking like a snake winding around the hillside as it climbed upward. Tall, towering ponderosa pines and sugar pines stood overlooking. Further up the road a few miles away was Iowa Hill, a place as rugged as the road that met it. About seven hundred people lived here at the turn of the century. The town was on the decline now, so different from its prosperous mining heyday in the 1850s and 1860s.

Lyman would settle north of the road near a place called Burnt Flat. He lived on a ranch with his brother Samuel who already had a job here. The ranch they lived on also wasn't very far from Dutch Flat. For extra money, the two young men cut firewood for people in the general area. Some people say they used a gas-powered cutter before there was such a thing.

As time went on, Lyman could be found with any one of his brothers gold or silver mining nearby, in a mine owned by their family or up in Dutch Flat as most settlers here became prospectors too.

With sands running through the hourglass and time running by, it was only fitting that the air pioneer would continue with his experiments. First, his flying materials were hauled to the area. The boy would then need financial help to continue his work. An Iowa Hill storekeeper, Tom Brown, gave him money to buy materials. His uncle Warren Gilmore and great-uncle Jack Gilmore would eventually help too.

Next, Lyman chose to work and continue his experiments in two places. Big Meadows became a lab of sorts where he would continue to build his aircraft and experiment with them. This was an area in El Dorado County and still not too far from where he lived.

A high cliff called Cape Horn would be used to test takeoffs for his gliders. Cape Horn Point was less than one mile from Colfax. The area was no ordinary place. Here, pine trees, sparse in number, grew from red clay and rock along the hillside. The tip of the horn itself had one of the grandest views of the countryside in the United States at the time. It sat on a mountain atop canyon ridges above the American River amid the high canyon walls. Rising air currents here would provide good conditions when testing and experimenting with his gliding craft. The area rested about a mile from Colfax and a mile due north of Burnt Flat. It was close to where the brothers lived.

Lyman continued his aviation study. He watched the birds and their movement in their natural habitat here. He wanted to test the gliders. One of the first things that Lyman, his brothers, and their friends had to do was to cut down trees to make landing sites available for the gliders to land. This was not always easy to do considering the number of tall evergreens and other trees in the general area.

The young inventor would then draw designs. The designs were always perfected with the four fundamental principles of flight in mind: motion, gravity, balance, and pressure. Then models were built, which were patterned after these designs.

Lyman experimented with the model gliders in different ways. Sometimes a cable-type wire would be strung down into the canyon and across the river. The experimental gliders would be pushed or just let go on the cable, leaving the winds to do the rest.

Now, rising air currents within the canyon and wind the gliders were riding against created air pressure underneath the wings. This helped support the engineless craft in the air. The forward-moving gliders would then fly higher. If the winds weren't just right, and sometimes it would get gusty, the gliders would teeter slightly before losing their balance and topple off the cable and into the river. Then Charles or Harrison or whoever was helping Lyman would go after the models and bring them back up the hill. Their dog would fetch them too. If Lyman's models flew successfully, the next step was to build larger craft patterned after the models. Then experiments would be done using the bigger models.

The young man developed a type of theory that he called the zigzag theory. This idea helped to explain what causes a glider to stay in the air. It is based on a law that affects motion and gravity at the same time to help a glider stay airborne by motion alone. He used the example of a leaf falling from a tree to the ground. When the leaf is falling in the air, it is pushed up from the air over and underneath it. The leaf naturally zigs or is tilted up on one side, but gravity pulls the leaf back down and tilts it to the other side creating a zag. This zigzag pattern continues until the leaf floats to the ground. Like the leaf, the glider zigs as a result of being lifted by the air but doesn't zag. It continues to move in one direction, stabilizing from its speed and power.

Lyman also experimented with weight and the placement of engines in various places on aircraft to balance them. One model was remote controlled and powered by clockworks. In Big Meadows, glider planes even having motors in them were tested. Some of the planes were also pushed down ramps and chutes. These experiments were done over and over again with many claiming they were completed with the utmost secrecy.

Now, some of the people who worked with Lyman in mines around the area had spent some of their own money to help him continue his experiments. They were getting upset that the inventor's experiments weren't successful right away. In fact, they laughed at him. They thought he was wasting his time thinking that he could get big models to fly.

Then in 1896, Lyman decided to test another glider. The glider had a propeller attached, and an engine was placed in the rear. Lyman's brothers, partners, and helpers constructed a wooden frame for a chute down the side of a hill. The plane would be pushed down the chute. In the beginning tests, all the plane could do was putt, stall, and fall to the ground.

He kept experimenting. His partners assisted him. After many practice tests, Lyman managed to get the plane up in the air. However, it became unmanageable and wobbly in windy weather. When the wind increased, it would throw the plane off balance causing it to make many crashes on the ground. Lyman's brothers and friends were becoming impatient with the planes' progress.

Then one day Lyman left his workshop camp. He went to a nearby hill observing the birds of the day flying then sleeping, noticing the nocturnal birds coming out at night. He realized that at sunset, the winds move in one direction; and at sunrise, the winds move in the opposite direction.

He then went back to experimenting. His friends and his brother Charles helped too. He still had no luck. The plane was wobbly as it flew. At one point, Lyman's helpers gave him one more day to work. If he wasn't successful, they were going to stop helping him. He decided to go back to the hill again. It was then that he had this vision, "I looked into the future, far as human eyes could see, beheld the bees and the birds and their dominion over the air; and I longed to do likewise, and then I saw a great airship, just like a mighty bird sailing o'er hills and mountains above the treetops and the clouds, with many human beings. All the faces I saw were smiling as it sped o'er the tops of trees and above the clouds to distant places without the buoyant bag of gas, which man was using to fly always. It had a cabin and great big engine, which I could clearly see was mounted in front of the cabin; and I heard the hum of its propellers die sway in the distance, o'er mountains and across the sea, like a swarm of angry bees. I saw ships of commerce sailing the seven seas, and I beheld ships of the air sailing to all parts of the earth." Lyman returned to camp. He created a makeshift cabin and fastened it to the glider. Then he took the engine from the rear of his glider plane and placed the engine ahead of the cabin just like the plane he saw in his vision. His helpers put a fifty-pound sandbag on the tail of the plane to balance the craft because the motor was now in front of the cabin. This still didn't seem to give the plane enough power to stay in the air.

The air pioneer was about ready to give up. He decided to give it one more try, only this time he took the sandbag off. "I pulled the throttle open, pulled the cord that cut the rope, that sent the plane down the chute . . . I could not look up," he said. "I waited for the crash but no crash, and the hum of the little propeller was now dying away. I realized something had happened. I peeked out from under my hat, and behold, the little plane was soaring away like a great bird . . . My big dog was after it by leaps and bounds." The powered glider is said to have sailed two hundred yards across the canyon to a perfect landing. Some say that Lyman's friends came out and threw up their hats at the discovery. At the end of the day, the men took the plane back to their shop.

Lyman Junior believed that he had solved the "eagle's secret" or what we know as the center of air pressure and gravity and the basics for aerodynamics. This secret of flight was based on how the birds fly. After realizing and understanding this idea, he started flying regularly and had much less trouble keeping his planes in the air.

Professor John Langley, the secretary of the Smithsonian Institution, was experimenting with planes about this time too. Mr. Langley and Lyman Junior corresponded from time to time. Lyman Junior wanted to help Mr. Langley balance his aircraft. It has been said that Mr. Langley refused. He didn't agree with the young man's balance theories and thought that all that was needed was better launching apparatus. It is recorded that Mr. Langley did have some success with a mechanically propelled air machine, which flew for some feet across the Potomac River.

In 1898, young Lyman designed and drew plans for a single-winged monoplane, with steel body, which allowed for passenger seating. These designs were based on the vision he had seen in 1896. This is believed to have been the idea for one of the early monoplanes and quite possibly the first drawing designed with passengers in mind. Many years later, he talked about experimenting to make this type of plane. When reflecting on his experiments done at Cape Horn, he told a news reporter in 1935, "It was here that we worked out the details of the plane that bears such a close resemblance to the planes of today. It was here that we conceived the thick-winged monoplane of passenger service." Many aviation pioneers up until this time were just experimenting with two-winged and three-winged planes.

The young man became interested in putting better motive power into his gliders. During 1902, he submitted a patent for a steam engine. Around this time, he constructed a thirty-two-foot glider equipped with a twenty-horsepower steam engine and flash boiler. He decided to try to fly his plane at a place called Knickerbocker Flat. On May 10, 1902, the 350-pound glider plane was pushed down an inclined chutelike ramp that was 100 yards long. Some say the chute was made of metal tubing or wood. The plane had skids instead of wheels. Upon leaving the chute, gravity forced the plane to speed up, causing it to go into the air and fly on its own for some distance on its own power. Some say the heavy boilers and furnaces kept it from climbing. This flight is known, in some circles, as the world's first powered glider flight. The monoplane glider made many flights from one hundred yards to one mile or more under perfect control. Twenty flights were listed in the inventor's logbook that year of 1902.

When experimenting, Lyman's planes often "made large circular flights and landed where they started." It is hard to say exactly when all these experiments took place. Recounts from the birdman's brothers and newspaper articles at the time place the dates between 1901 and 1906.

One thing is for sure: Lyman and Charles, the brother who helped with so many of the experiments, liked to have their dog along. The mutt loved to chase after the planes and sometimes help fetch them too. The two brothers also liked to go to Colfax to do their business because it was so close to Cape Horn.

Later, Lyman wrote to the United States War Department urging the government to build an air fleet that would help in time of war. A simple air fleet of only about six planes existed then. He realized that it needed to grow to help our country's security. In fact, he was so sure of his ideas that he called himself an aerial Fulton.

Now the Wright brothers and Professor Langley had airplane-testing fields. However, Lyman kept thinking about the idea that people, mail, and cargo could be transported by planes. Remember that a few years earlier at the ranch near Red Bluff, he tried to make a plane for delivering mail.

By this time, the railroad was touting itself with the greatest of glory in being the foremost mode of transportation. The Never Come Never Go Narrow Gauge railroad line ran through the local area. Lyman had even helped to build a bridge so the rails could run through here. In 1902 he also began talking to the people at the railroad station in the city of Colfax, trying to convince them that it was conceivable to carry mail by air as well as by rail. Remember again that from the 1860s until now, much of the nation's mail was usually carried by steamer or the train lines. Lyman somehow believed that there was still a better, faster way to have it done.

As always, financial backing was very important to the young inventor's endeavors. The next year, Lyman decided to give his first public flight exhibition near Cape Horn. Whether fact or legend, some onlookers later recalled that a plane flew about three miles, returned, and alighted at the top of the hill from where it started. Ways to raise more money to help him build a larger machine were set into motion. Onlookers, impressed by the flight, circulated a petition; and $1,700 was raised to build a larger machine. However, not every event that happened that day was in Lyman's favor. The clever mayor of a nearby town also tried raising money to help by staging an old-fashioned holdup on the outskirts of town that day. Two masked bandits took money and jewels from people riding the stagecoaches. Toward evening, the mayor felt he couldn't continue his little scheme to gather more money and told the townspeople, "Gentlemen, to show you we were merely staging a show, I hand you back your money and jewels." It seems that the people didn't appreciate the mayor's trick, and they refused to give Lyman any money for the show or his planes. It took him many months to get people interested in his planes again. Now he was afraid to fly and display them before the public.

Lyman Junior invented a carbide lighting system for houses and hotels in 1905. In fact, he used this lighting system to light his own house during a time when he lived in Colfax. His brothers said years later that he installed systems in the houses of nearby cities. That same year, the United Bank and Trust Company of Sacramento promised to give money to help him. He wanted to continue experimenting with his gliders and planes. The inventor, his brother, and helpers were going to need a larger and more open area and landing site. Lyman also continued to think about building an airship based on his 1896 vision of a cabin monoplane carrying passengers across the sky. He had a wonderful plan.

Chapter Four

The Airfield and the Gilmore Airship Company

The city of Grass Valley, like Iowa Hill and Colfax, had been a well-known mining town during the gold rush. It was located about fifteen miles west of Colfax. The name of the city originated from events of a local legend about some early pioneers who were led by their hungry cows from a well-populated route north at Truckee to a "grassy valley" around 1848. Later, some miners camping along the Bear River found gold in the streambed of Wolf Creek. In 1849, some people from Boston built a few cabins near the creek. A Frenchman here set up a trade post. Though it was winter, the primitive makings of the town began. In the 1850s, there was a post office, hotels, and saloons. The town's first newspaper office had been operating since the 1870s. By 1905, there were mines operating here, and some logging was helping the economy of the city.

Within two years' time, Lyman and two companions, J. S. Goodwin and Leroy M. Clark, moved to Grass Valley from Colfax and began glider experiments.

Sometime before 1907, Lyman Junior began to create enthusiasm for an airfield. He started telling others about his ideas. Some very influential people in the gold business promised to help him with his ventures. Businessmen in nearby Sacramento were interested in the building of a flying machine. Also, gold miners in the local area thought it would be a good idea too. They believed that an "air machine" would be very helpful in transporting gold bullion mined in the area to the mint in San Francisco. In Grass Valley, there were foundries where Lyman could cast metals used for making plane parts. Engine shops also existed here at the time. This, along with the need to store the craft he had in mind, prompted him to choose a piece of land just outside the mountain mining town.

In the beginning, this had not been an easy task for young Gilmore who had investigated seven areas. Some of these places were located in different counties in California, and each one had characteristics suitable for an airport. In the local area, a place called Glenbrook was considered, but a high south wind and low north wind would make plane takeoffs and landings unsafe. A location near the highway, which ran between Grass Valley and Colfax, may have worked; but a place called Osborn Hill protected the area from winds. This would create air moving beneath and in a different direction than the regular air currents, thus making flight in and out of the location hazardous. One field atop a long high-rising hill within the city limits was considered.

Undertow currents there would not make it safe for flying. Finally, he settled on a place called the Woods Tract because there were uniform rising air currents from each direction, which would help planes to take off and land into the wind. Also, the location was above the tule fog with easy access to major highways and other city locations.

Even though the winds and location were adequate, there were other problems to challenge young Gilmore in his desire to create an airfield here. Only a few trees were growing along the outside perimeter of the field. However, the location of the land was close to a town with nearby houses. The structures might block airspace that would be needed for incoming and outgoing planes. The runway itself was humped so that landing on the airstrip would not be easy. Also, clumps of weeds created small mounds over the entire area. Masses of dust could create problems for future planes and pilots too. Finally, the field was relatively small with not enough land for expanding in future years.

Nevertheless, the young man proceeded to create a primitive runway here calling this his "airship camp." The camp assumed the formal name the Gilmore Flying Field and officially opened on a rainy March 15, 1907.

Lyman also designed a map. This drawing detailed elements of an airfield that was established in 1908. Planes would be able to land from any direction onto the center of the field where a white circle could be seen. A wind sock was placed atop a pole that stood in or near the circle to make it more easily seen from the air.

The plans also included runways that ran in different directions. The east-west runway would be two thousand feet with a prevailing wind coming from the west in the summer and southeast in the winter. The southeast-northwest runway would be 1,700 feet with a prevailing wind from the southeast in the wintertime. The southwest-northeast runway would have a length of 1,600 feet with a prevailing southwest wind in the fall and spring. Extensions to the runways would be added in time as they were needed. The runways would provide for the taking off and landing of planes from all points. A flight line area where planes would park was also indicated.

A power line that had been arranged to be built before Lyman started building the field would also eventually be in the way of planes coming in or going out. The building of the power line proceeded upon the agreement that as soon as the airfield grew and more airspace was needed, the line would be removed. Also, oiling the field would help mat down the large amounts of dust, which had accumulated there.

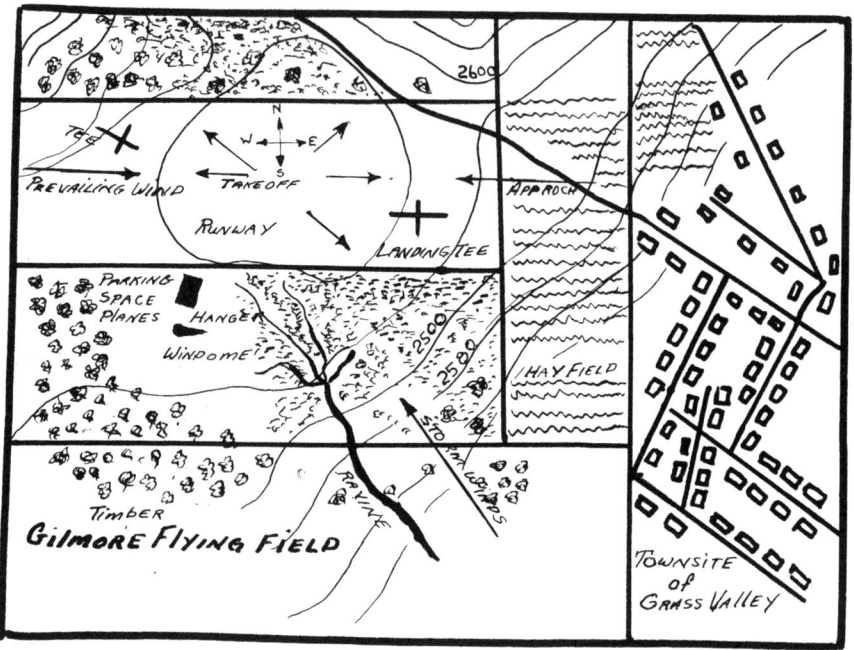

At some time, a wooden barnlike building was built for a hangar. The hangar would be called the Gilmore Aerodrome. There is some speculation about whether the hangar was built in Red Bluff where Lyman spent his younger days. The more popular belief is that the hangar was built right here on the Gilmore Field. Business soon started inside the hangar. Lyman and his brother Charles began building a big monoplane. The plane would have a single engine and would be based on the designs that Lyman had drawn in 1898. A cabin would be built in the new mechanical bird that was encased in a metal fuselage about the size of an automobile. It would be big enough to hold eight passengers. In front of the cabin would be an enclosed cockpit.

As building of the plane progressed, other features were noticeable. The plane itself had retractable landing gear. It weighed about twenty-four hundred pounds. Numerous bracelike struts were added to help release the pressure of the weight of the plane and to hold it up. The unwieldy invention was thirty-five feet long. Its giant wings resembled those of an eagle and spanned sixty-five feet.

Now Lyman's shop was a busy place. Many parts for the airship were handmade. It has been said that the machines in the shop operated on a type of solar power and would only run on a warm summer day. Fifty-gallon drums were used perhaps holding water to generate electricity.

At times, Charles was the main mechanic helping to build parts for the plane. He would also help clean the wings of the big monoplane by sweeping the dust off with a broom. As always, Lyman and Charles loved the friendship of their dog. The dog liked to climb up onto and inside the plane while the brothers worked in the shop.

It has been said that by this time, Lyman Junior's father realized how serious his son really was about flying and that he even sewed fabric on the wings of the giant monoplane. Unlike the Irish linen used on wings of Lyman's later planes, muslin was used to create the wings of this one.

The brothers wore their mining clothes most of the time. A small miner's hat, vests, boots, and trousers were typical clothes they liked to wear. Showing off their independence, the Gilmores wore shoulder-length hair even in their later years, which was not at all common by then.

The two liked the location of their workplace. For one thing, the stars twinkled brightly on many nights. They believed the crisp, clean mountain air was healthy and would result in one living a long life.

Now, Lyman continued experimenting with the big monoplane he had nicknamed Big Betsy in honor of a favorite niece. By this time, he was substituting gas engines in planes instead of the more dangerous steam engines. To save money, he used a motor that was used in balloons. It was the first Durak motor sold in the United States by Alberto Santos Dumont. After testing, it was found that the motor was not powerful enough to turn the large propeller of the giant plane.

Some say there was a fire here in 1907. A flaming candle set on a stand near a sleeping workman was the culprit. Nobody knows much more than that.

Later, the airman created another monoplane. The craft, smaller in size, weighed about 1,600 pounds. Some say it was built to carry four passengers. Others proclaim that Lyman built it to carry just himself or himself and another passenger. It was similar in design to the Curtis Robin planes, which flew forty years later. The plane was controlled by pulling wires attached to various points on the flexible wings. It had an open cockpit.

This plane was built to fit the motor that wasn't working in the big monoplane. Lyman had to repair the engine taken from the big plane and install it in the little monoplane. After trial tests of the makeshift engine, it was found that it was not powerful enough to make the little plane operate successfully.

The designs for both planes were like those of no others created by air pioneers of the day. Most people believe the little monoplane was built in 1907 or 1908. However, it was still being tested in 1912. Lyman would boast that the big monoplane was built around 1907 or 1908. Whatever the true date of their building, both were new ideas in airplane construction.

In 1908, Lyman also submitted to the U.S. patent office an application for a water cooler, filter, purifier, and storage apparatus. It was witnessed by two people. Around this time, he also invented the rotary snowplow for use by the railroads. Later, this invention would be used to help clear roads during snowstorms.

The next year, the birdman invited a few citizens from the area to witness one of his experimental flights back at Cape Horn near Colfax. Two successful flights were made from the cape. The tin craft that was used in the experiment had a five-foot wingspan and seemed to perform incredible maneuvers on its own. Like magic, regardless of how the plane was dropped, tail first or upside down, after falling about twenty feet, the craft would automatically right itself and level off flying across the river and return to its starting place. Those who watched the experiment noticed that the craft was able to fly without spinning or crashing. It had a gyroscope that was operated by a storage battery. The battery itself was able to stay charged to its full capacity by a secret electrical influence. During one flight, the metal plane flew for 3,000 feet at an altitude of 250 feet. It flew for six hundred feet and as high as fifty feet in another test flight.

Now, it seems that this plane was so popular that the state fair officials in Sacramento wanted Lyman to display it each day during the fair at Agricultural Park. Nobody really knew all the details about how the plane worked, and Lyman kept this a secret. The newspaper said that when performing at the fair, this demonstration plane made circles, rose higher into the air, and dropped, then returned to where it started. Some people say that a shift in winds that day kept the experiment from being entirely successful.

Lyman and some Colfax businessmen wanted to build a bigger flying machine based on the design of this plane. However, they would need money to build it. In order to do this, Lyman, his brother Samuel, D. A. Russel (a cattleman), and a county official founded the Colfax Aeroplane Company. Mr. Matteson would be company president.

Within a few days, the beginnings of the company were started in Colfax. Mr. Gilmore would begin to make his transactions for the company through the Colfax Bank. Immediately he began to sell shares of stock that were sold for $1 each in the form of certificates. The townspeople purchased these. Money the company accumulated from the stock certificates would be donated for the construction of an airplane for demonstration as well as marketing purposes.

In the meantime, something happened to the metal plane. Lyman had hid the plane in a mine shaft so that no one would find out how it worked. A newspaper said that it had been tampered with and been stolen. Unfortunately, around fair time, Lyman was walking back to a cabin he had near Iowa Hill and noticed fragments of clockworks of his plane strewn along the ground.

Now, the airman really believed in his new company, and he still wanted to build a plane based on the design of the stolen plane and build other planes. However, his partners weren't sure that he would complete the designs for his planes.

Lyman decided to take matters into his own hands. In February of 1910, he reinvented the company. The Colfax Aeroplane Company was newly incorporated into the Gilmore Airship Company. Lyman Junior's new partners included two of his brothers, an attorney, a bank president, and a county recorder. D. A. Russel, the cattleman from Colfax, joined the group. Ivan Parker, a county official, became president of the company. Other investors included J. S. Goodwin, known as the Hydraulic King, Lewis Clark from the town of You Bet and Red Dog, and others from Sacramento and San Francisco who were interested in his experiments. The stockholders would meet each year in Colfax. Townspeople in the local area would continue to buy stock certificates for $1 a share.

In 1910, the Gilmore Industrial Syndicate was also formed to help market Lyman's many gadgets and inventions. Lyman's cousin, neighbor, and overseer of his company Mr. Clark became a partner in the association. The Hydraulic King, Mr. Goodwin, joined the undertaking.

Other aviation pioneers and aeronauts were experimenting around this time too. However, experimenting with planes and gliders was dangerous. Some weren't as lucky as Lyman. In 1911, a man named John Montgomery died when his Evergreen glider crashed on Montgomery Hill in San Jose, California. That same year, Robert Fowler, a pilot trained by the Wright brothers, tried to fly his Wright Model B plane over the Sierra Nevada. He wanted to win a $50,000 prize to be the first man to fly from San Francisco to New York. Due to a sudden gust of wind, the aircraft shook, causing it to fall apart at a place called Carpenter's Flat near Alta and not far from Dutch Flat. Some have said that Lyman told Mr. Fowler that it would be far too dangerous and that he needed clearings for planes to land. Mr. Fowler didn't heed the warning, and his plane crashed.

In the meantime, Lyman really believed in the Gilmore Airship Company. The experiments continued. About this time, he held a simple flight demonstration at Gilmore Field. A few people came to see him work. A small plane had been tied to the ground inside his shop so that it wouldn't shoot up through the roof of the hangar. When the thirty-five-horsepower motor was started in the craft, the crankshaft snapped in two, sending pieces of the engine and other debris flying through the shop.

Unfortunately, by this time, some miners and other supporters had long deserted Lyman's ideas and experiments. His partners were not very supportive either. They were getting impatient with his repeated failed attempts to get a plane off the ground and his desire for expensive equipment. The partners didn't realize that most motors at that time weren't powerful enough to lift planes of such magnitude. By this time, the company had already invested $8,000 in his planes. Even with growing skepticism, Lyman continued to experiment and test.

In 1912, D. E. Matteson, a brick and stone mason, was president of the Gilmore Airship Company. The stockholders that year agreed to buy another engine. This one would accompany the little monoplane. The engine would cost $2,600 and was later believed to be a seventy-five-horsepower Roberts engine. Maybe this engine would turn the plane's propeller creating enough power to lift it up. The members also elected a new director that year who would also be the business manager for the company. Lyman would now work under the business manager. He was now not even in control of his own company.

Meanwhile, he continued to test the little monoplane. Some say one day, while wheeling around the field, the little plane hit a huge boulder on the field, causing the propeller to crack. Another time, when taking the small plane out for a balance test, Lyman made an attempt to fly it. After several tries, the plane was up a few feet off the ground when a gust of wind redirected it into some pine trees. Lyman turned the plane's power off. As a result, the airship managed to land in a pile of rocks. With its propeller slowly grinding in the dirt, the plane managed to swirl around, splitting one of its wings. With bent and crooked axles, it turned and tilted and was a little over a foot off the ground when it landed in the runway in a heap with Lyman imprisoned in the seat. He realized after all his tests, however, that the plane was still too large and heavy for the engine. Poor Lyman experienced many crashes. Several torn wings, torn-off landing gear, bent propellers and plane bellies, smashed wings, and crooked airplane axles were results of his trial-and-error endeavors. Mishap after mishap occurred, but he didn't seem to be bothered by it all. The experiments went on. Attempt after attempt to run the machines and the struggle to lift them up was made. A few came to see the man continue his seemingly futile tests.

Now, most people say that the big monoplane never flew. They say that Lyman never flight-tested it because no engine could accommodate it. There were doubts that it ever left the hangar. It may have also been used as a demonstration plane to show to investors.

It is believed that the small monoplane did not fly either. The little air machine taxied around the field. The best it could do was to make leaps and jumps and lift off the ground for a few feet at a time. However, some people believed it did fly. It has been said that at a later date, this plane with a forty-five-foot wingspan made short flights after it was installed with a powerful-enough motor. The wings of the aircraft resembled those of a bat. In fact, it was called a bat-wing plane, and the nickname "bat plane" was started.

A newspaper reported that one summer evening, the air pioneer made a trial flight in an aircraft of his own invention. Some people who witnessed the flight said that the plane managed to leave the white circle from his airstrip at Gilmore Field and fly five feet or so off the ground for about one-half mile. About the same time, Lyman also gave a small exhibition at Gilmore Field. He had his planes lined up for a few onlookers to see. During this time, mining activities began to take up much of his time.

According to legend, the Gilmore Industrial Syndicate, which had been formed three years earlier, met its greatest challenge in 1913. A difference of opinion came about as to what resources the company should use. Mr. Goodwin wanted to continue hydraulic mining in the area. This type of mining was outlawed around these parts at this time. Clark did not want to do business this way. Then the bickering started. Mr. Clark and some acquaintances, as well as Mr. Goodwin, happened to be at a miner's cabin in the town of You Bet. The men all started drinking. Mr. Goodwin told everyone to leave the cabin, shooting the walls as they left. Three days later, Mr. Clark returned to the cabin. The two men figured to put an end to the squabbling. There was a shootout. Both men were gone to their graves by morning, thus ending the industrial syndicate. Lyman began to take care of Mr. Clark's wife, Marie, who was now a widow.

Chapter Five

The Inventor's Other Businesses

The years from 1914 to 1918 were uncertain ones in America. World War I was raging. During these years, the United States government set up different administrations to control the price and usage of our nation's fuel, food, and manufactured goods. Some goods were starting to be taxed including telephone and telegraph services. Millions of dollars were used to send food and supplies to soldiers overseas. Financing the war effort was everyone's first concern.

During this time, Lyman wrote to his mother, saying, "I'm still working on inventions, but nothing as yet has come through; all things seem to stand still and wait for cash to promote them with. I have several men working to raise cash money, but it is hard to get finances during the war."

In 1916, Lyman was working on plans for a small wartime submarine "chaser." He wanted to give the United States Navy his idea. He sent his idea to the government. When he didn't get a reply, he wrote to President Wilson who wrote back saying his idea accidentally got lost. Lyman and Charles continued as woodcutters for the local area during this time. People would buy the four-foot lengths of wood they cut.

In 1916 and 1917, the Gilmore brothers made an agreement with the public and signed a contract to form a corporation to manufacture inventions and to develop mineral land. After all, Lyman had become known in industrial circles by now. He was considered to be an expert mechanic frequently called upon by the local railroad and others to perform difficult repairs on motor cars and machinery of intricate construction. Along with the airfield, he had invented other types of machines and some he tried to patent. Some of the money the company made would pay for developing mining property that Lyman was interested in at the time. This Blue Channel Mining property lay within the Iowa Hill Mining District. Some of the money would also go to help power the machines at the Gilmore Airship Company. Company shares would be sold for 10¢ a share.

Sometime in 1918 the two brothers bought a house in Nevada City, four miles north of Grass Valley. Parts of machines and mechanical devices both old and new lay in tall stacks throughout the house, some reaching as high as the ceiling. Narrow paths cleared the way for one to walk through.

Despite the war, Lyman continued improving his planes and continued to work with small glider models too. As always, the experiments continued, and he built more planes at Gilmore Airfield. In fact, he built twenty planes during his career as an aviation pioneer. Other hangars were eventually built to house these planes. These hangars bordered the runways as the area began to look like an airpark.

Unlike modern airfields, a plane from somewhere else would land here only once in a great while. Also, most flight activities at the field up to this time were kept away from the public. However, youngsters and others wandering on the property at times couldn't resist an occasional peek through the windows and cracks in the walls of the hangars to catch a glimpse of the objects inside.

After the war, the air pioneer engaged the use of hired pilots who kept the townspeople entertained by doing tricks in the air with the planes. They say that some of the pilots were famous fliers. Lyman would also roll out his flying machines from the hangars and display them alongside the runways for the public to see. People would park their buggies and picnic while watching the air shows.

During the postwar years, Lyman also purchased army planes used in the war for training pilots at his airfield. There were also planes of other makes and models that were seen at Gilmore Field.

By 1920, other plane companies were using Gilmore Field. Among them was the Mattley Airplane and Motor Company of Marysville. The company was giving demonstration rides to local people at the field and was considering supplying the nearby mines by air.

In the next few years, Lyman turned some of his energy toward his mining interests in Iowa Hill. After all, these claims helped him when he needed money for his projects. One of the properties he managed was right in town. It was called the Blue Channel Mine. This was a very rich gravel gold-producing district of the famous Blue Land Channel. Unfortunately, Iowa Hill's mining boom had already started to decline. The big booming years for this area had been from 1853 to 1865. However, Lyman who was strongly determined in everything he did continued to try to find gold here.

In 1921, he broke into a channel that was the feeder into the old Morning Star and Big Dipper mines of the general area. These mines had created about $3 million from about 1901 until 1906 and made four men very rich indeed. Seymour Waterhouse became wealthy from the Big Dipper Mine. Ex-lieutenant governor J. H. Neff and John and Ed Cloman all became wealthy from the Morning Star Mine. Lyman had hopes for these mines to forfeit as much gold.

Snow fell in Colfax during the last week of June and the first week of July that year. Many boys and girls and grown-ups too celebrated the arrival by making snowmen and enjoyed the sport of throwing snowballs.

In 1922, Lyman and a promoter purchased the General Grant Placer Mine near Iowa Hill. He then opened a drain tunnel that same year to free water within the two thousand miles of tunnels and crosscuts, making it easier to get to some high-grade ore that had been found.

His mining interests didn't stop here. The man invented a gold-saving device that caught the attention of the local miners. When demonstrating it to them one day, Lyman made a bet with a miner that the machine would separate the gold from the dirt. He started up the machine. The gold was then hurried to the county assayer's office. Six ounces of gold had been separated from the soil!

In 1924, he sold his Blue Channel Mine property that was then developed into a formal group called the Providence Quartz Mining Group that same year.

Meanwhile, Lyman continued his enthusiasm and was interested in creating other airstrips, this time taking his interests to Iowa Hill. The Boeing Airport Company asked the United States Commerce Department for permission to build an emergency landing strip with an airport in this area, along the divide, so that airplane flight over the Sierra Nevada would be safer. This area was above the fog, and pilots would be able to see the light from beacons in Sacramento, Marysville, or any valley point. Also, some planes flying over the area had been lost. It was believed that an airport here could also prevent plane accidents. The mild weather in this area would mean that an airport could be opened year-round.

Now, the local chamber of commerce was only three years old that same year. Lyman Gilmore Jr. and a pilot named Mr. Virden attended a meeting to discuss the issue of having a landing field for airplanes in the area.

In 1925, Lyman and his partners wanted to help by building a nine-mile road from Colfax to Iowa Hill so it could act as an airstrip and the beginnings of an airport there. He approached the county board of supervisors later in 1928 requesting the building of the road. He even told them he would match up to $12,000 in funds if the county would help him. The board told him there was not enough county money. The many attempts to build a field or airport here proved futile. The project didn't get off the ground. The idea wasn't taken seriously by some who thought that there wasn't enough level ground in this area to develop an airfield.

Even though stories in later years talked of Lyman flying many distances, a newspaper reported that he, along with the guidance of his pilot Mr. Virden, piloted a regular plane for the first time that year. On this day, the plane was described as flying haphazardly over Colfax and North Bloomfield, flying low and dipping down toward the buildings and trees. People complained about the occurrence. This was quite a common reaction from people in early days of flying. What a thrill it must have been for Lyman, though, poking out the cockpit into the open air with no roof to hamper his curiosity and view—to feel the shaking and rattling of this birdlike metal machine!

Around this time, he also took a young man riding in his plane to see how his hometown looked from the clouds. The *Covered Wagon* happened to be the big feature film in town during the falltime of that year.

Chapter Six

Mr. Gilmore's Older Years

Lyman's creative thinking continued to help him in his struggle to keep the airfield in Grass Valley growing. In 1927, he advertised upcoming events at his field in the newspaper. During that year, the air pioneer tried to accumulate enough money to build some planes, exhibition planes as they were called, and keep them at the airfield until they were paid in full. He then sold them to be used in other cities in California.

He also made up and typed an agreement to form a new company called the Gilmore United Airways Company. Mr. Gilmore "wanted a properly organized United Airway concern where every town and city" throughout the state might take part in commercial aviation and have airplanes and landing fields at their command.

An advertisement for airplane rides at Gilmore Field appeared in the local paper in the springtime of 1927. Rides were being offered to the public during certain hours for short or distance flights by the now-named Gilmore Aviation Company. Two people could take a ride in a plane for a charge of $5. Longer flights would cost 10¢ a mile.

That same year, Lyman attended an aeronautical conference at the Hotel Whitcomb in San Francisco. Most of the people there did not know who he was. A newspaper report about the conference stated that "some of the old-timers knew him and crowded around to shake his hand . . . it seems certain that this strange-appearing man bears the distinction of being a pioneer in aviation and one whose experiments have helped to advance the science of flying."

In 1928, some buyers were considering moving a big monoplane from Gilmore Field to Mills Field in San Francisco in hopes of putting it on public exhibition there. People could view the monoplane for 25¢.

The United States stock market crashed the following year in 1929. The nation's economy started becoming weak and sick. "Relief" was given to poor people; and everyone volunteered to help their neighbors, friends, and those in need. It was a hard time to be an American because most people had very little money.

The year proved to be a good one, though, and even a milestone, for the airfield. In October, an airport flier from Oakland, California, landed a cabin airplane at Gilmore Field for the first time. It was also in 1929 that years of Lyman's efforts came full circle as the Grass Valley City Council established the Gilmore Airfield as a municipal airport. It was named the Grass Valley Airport. At this time, Lyman spent hours at his drawing board working on plans for a large transport plane. He claimed that this plane would have a nine thousand-mile cruising radius.

The next decade of the 1930s would pose as a challenging one for Mr. Gilmore. In 1930, he was back circulating and accumulating petitions signed by the townspeople of the Colfax Iowa Hill area then submitting them to the county board of supervisors. This was a step he took in trying to get a field built here that would act as a training area for gliders, particularly for use by the local high schools to be used by young aviators. By now, he had spent a lot of time exposing the public to his interest in trying to get other flying fields established. He had also volunteered his expertise, time, and money to further the growth of aviation especially on the West Coast.

Sadly, Lyman soon became a victim in many ways. In 1931, Marie Clark, a caretaker of orphans and the woman who had befriended him for eighteen years, died. The following year, a newspaper reported that a log cabin he owned in Iowa Hill had gone up in smoke. The fire was caused by sparks from the chimney igniting the roof.

A big monoplane was being taken apart at the airfield in 1935 so that it could be taken to the Chicago World's Fair to be reassembled for exhibition that year. Unfortunately, many wooden buildings of that time couldn't withstand the vagaries of fire. Fire struck the airport. Lyman Gilmore Jr.'s hangars, shop, planes, and tools burned to the ground. Among the planes burned were some old ones that an Eastern museum was interested in displaying. Handmade turnbuckles, landing gear from a big monoplane, parts of turbines from his steam engine, and a model plane were some of the few remnants remaining. Unbelievably, a tree, nicknamed the Old Oak Tree, which grew and weathered the years as the airship company operated, remained standing. Some say a forest fire caused the blaze or that it was the result of an argument. Still, others have their doubts and believe the fire was mysterious.

One of Mr. Gilmore's houses on Aristocracy Hill in Nevada City also burned down that year. His office was in this house. Numerous drawings and records were also destroyed. Many of his designs, drawings, and pictures pulled from the house were taken nearby to another house he owned that was still standing. The artifacts lay in piles. Fortunately, his most treasured designs had been kept in a safe-deposit box at the bank. Other documents relating to his precious inventions were stored there too.

What a devastating event to happen to this courageous mountain man who filled his life with experiments in aviation. This air pioneer affectionately called Eagle of the Sierras would never again build a plane.

After 1935, Lyman continued to draw plans at his home in Nevada City, California. His vision included the construction of a working model of an individual-type plane with folding wings and the ground operating facilities of an automobile. He was also working on improving plane motors. Some say he continued drawing airplane engine designs. Some of these were of big passenger planes flying thousands of miles without refueling. He continued to invent gadgets, and he also kept working with local businessmen.

In the latter part of the decade, some Hollywood stars began to finance one of Lyman's mines only to take control of it for a while. After court entanglements, which lasted six years, Lyman regained ownership of his mine. One day the Santos Gang, believing that one of Lyman's mines had riches, approached and threatened him about taking over the mine. Luckily, Lyman convinced them there was no treasure here, and the gang left.

In the decade between 1940 and 1950, the circumstances in the remaining years of Lyman's life continued to have a sad note. His Blue Channel Mine did not bring forth the gold he once thought it would. The tragedy of losing the airfield and little progress in his mining claims left him a poor man. Some people say that he even burnt tires to keep warm. So saddened by the loss, he would go to the airfield and rummage through the remains of his burnt planes. Some have said that Lyman would stand on the street corners and tell people that someday airplanes would carry two hundred passengers at a time back and forth across the oceans. He would also talk about trips to the moon and Mars.

The scientific community hadn't completely forgotten about him though. He was now receiving a small amount of money from the Daniel Guggenheim Foundation. While studying seabirds, and particularly seagulls, in his younger years on jaunts to the ocean, he discovered an important idea. He noticed in the seagull that the "thickness of the wing was one-eighth that of its distance from the leading edge to the trailing edge." Knowing this helped Lyman to design and build wings that had better lift. The stipend from the foundation was also to reward him for his efforts in promoting aviation along the West Coast.

In the following years, the newspapers were showcasing fewer headlines and news of his lauded flight trials. People were talking about the automobile, the newest and most popular invention of the day. Using the airplane for carrying mail and commercial passengers was still a new idea.

Sadly, progress of Lyman Junior's tests already handicapped by financial struggles and now challenged by this unforeseen fire was now changed forever. By now, other local fields had opened up to provide plane flight for emergency use for fire planes. Soon, other aviation explorers were beginning to make progress in their own experiments with flight.

The Great Depression ended in 1941. That was the same year that America entered into World War II. During the war years, Lyman told President Franklin Roosevelt and Secretary of State Winston Churchill about his ideas for a torpedo device that would help win the war.

Lyman's brother Charles never married. Charles, the brother who had been the main mechanic in the airfield shop for years and assisted Lyman in so many of his experiments and ventures, died four years later in 1945.

In 1946, Lyman was a special guest at an air circus along with local and state officials. This affair was given to benefit an airport in Nevada City. Air circuses were held in different places during this time. Flight races and exhibitions at these circuses were held for the public to see. The following year, he was honored for his contributions with a plaque from California's governor Warren.

In 1951, Lyman got very sick. His brothers Elmer and Sam moved into his Nevada City home to live with him. Later, when Lyman was hospitalized with his illness, he was reluctant to give up his longtime beard when nurses had to shave it off for medical reasons.

The visionary pioneer who never gave up despite the many obstacles he faced died from a stroke on February 23, 1951, at the Nevada County Hospital in Nevada City, California.

Chapter Seven

Remembering the Air Pioneer

There are a few people living today who remember Lyman Gilmore Jr. or "Gil" as his friends and helpers called him. They say that Lyman and three of his brothers were bachelors all of their lives.

One citizen remembers a story about Lyman Gilmore Jr. that she recalls as a little girl living in Colfax. She tells the story about the day when the kids in her family were coming home from the movies. Their house was situated behind the theater in town with a yard or fence in between them. The children passed the family woodshed and opened the back door to the kitchen. She chuckles when she remembers how surprised her brother was as he saw Lyman Gilmore Jr. sitting at the kitchen table talking with the rest of the family. She remembers her brother's reaction when he noticed a big lump on Lyman's head but doesn't remember him telling them how he got it. The children were huddled by the kitchen stove as Lyman Gilmore Jr. talked to her father. She recalls that Mr. Gilmore never creased the black hat that he wore as was the proper thing to do with hats then . . . Instead, he wore it in a narrow rounded fashion on his head. Lyman was said to have been quite shy. He was bald during his later years and is seen wearing a hat in some of his photographs.

For many years, the air pioneer continued to cut wood in the local area, providing four-foot lengths to a school district.

People remember that he had a funny old car. In fact, he had several makes of old cars. Some of the names people have mentioned that may have been among them are LaSalle, Studebaker, and Peerless. Some were clunkers that he liked to fix up himself. During the World War II years, he would drive one of his cars around the Colfax Iowa Hill area. He would load it up with two gallons of gasoline, five gallons of kerosene, and off he would go.

Several stories have been passed down throughout the years about Lyman's scruffy beard that he reportedly started growing when he was thirty-five. One story is that he caught the influenza in Alaska. A doctor told him that his beard would help him to get better. Others say that Lyman boasted about keeping the beard on until William Jennings Bryan became president. This never happened, so the beard stayed on!

Lyman always wore a suit, sometimes taking off his coat in the summertime. During his later years, he liked to wear a long battered black coat all the time. True or not, one story is told over and over again that $15,000 was sewn into the lining of the coat! That's why he always wore it.

He was thought of as colorful and quite a character to some. For others, his shy, modest demeanor seemed to stand out. Many remember the lonely odd man's love for storytelling and joking with people. Some who didn't understand Lyman said he was strange, that in his older years, he was crotchety and had an eccentric nature, especially after Marie Clark's death.

Even so, Lyman Gilmore Jr. was partially responsible for the beginnings of commercial airfields and airports as we know them today. Instead of using his field just for testing, he also used the formal elements of modern airports on the land. There was a distinct takeoff and landing point. His plans included a specific area for taxiing and parking planes. His planes were specifically built with passengers in mind. He built new planes too. Other makes and models of planes could be seen at his airfield, and pilots from other places came to visit. He is also said to have had a "scanty air service, which kept business alive" for a short period.

This adventurer was ahead of his time. Some say that he foresaw the day when people used the airplane in everyday life and that the passenger plane would be as popular as the automobile. He also realized that the airplane could someday be used for mass transportation. One newspaper article written about Lyman in 1924 said that he had a plan to maintain a regular service from the local area to surrounding points and to gradually develop along lines indicated by aviation development. Among his early writings were records found that also showed he had a general plan to establish an airline service that would connect cities and towns in California and throughout the United States while delivering "mail, supplies, and even people quickly, dependably, and economically."

He helped establish airfields for airmail too. "I gave much assistance to the men at work establishing the airlines and airfields for mail service and gave land for a field," he said.

Ideas for small private planes as we know them today were also in his vision for the future. "The day will come," he said, "when flying autos will enable men and women to have their homes in any city or high up in the mountains, miles from where they work. It will be a simple matter to fly from the country to town, alight, fold your wings, and drive to your parking place."

Flying for pleasure, flying for the businessman who values his time and utilizes the airplane to get to a destination quickly, delivering light parcels and mail was how air transportation would evolve in the years to come according to Mr. Gilmore.

Many say that the designs of Lyman Gilmore's planes were sophisticated compared to other planes built in his day and age. He is thought to have been the first person to depart from the double-wing plane to the single-wing, low-type airplane. His theories of monoplane wing design were used for many years after they were developed. Also, other inventors had toyed with the idea of pusher-typed planes with the pilot's seat pitched out in front, but the enclosed cabin was a step ahead of this in vision and for practical use. Again, he may have been first to advocate aluminum-covered wings and retractable landing gear for aircraft. The retractable landing gear seen in his 1898 drawings were used on transport ships in the 1930s.

Some honorable character traits also led to Lyman Gilmore Jr.'s success. One of his outstanding qualities was a commitment to involvement in the community. He took an active role in trying to make his community a better place to live. He was a member of local organizations and the chamber of commerce. His participation in helping to build his community was noticed by the many newspaper articles appearing at the time describing his experiments and projects.

However, the man's genius was misunderstood. Neighbors and friends would sometimes ridicule or make fun of his ideas. In order to defend himself, Lyman would tell funny tales about his works. He endured many setbacks during his career including lack of money, interest in his projects, and scorn from others. This didn't stop the historical inventor from trying to reach his goals. If one of his experiments didn't work, he would try another.

Today, there remain many unanswered questions about Lyman Gilmore Jr.'s experiments and his flying success. This may be due to the fact that like other explorers of his day, he did not realize how important his accomplishments might be to future generations. Many aviation pioneers in that time unfortunately did not record their experiments and flight tests.

His aeronautical career also happened during a time when everyone wanted to be first to fly. Fierce competition within the aeronautical community made progress for any one individual difficult. Some pilots were claiming that their ideas about wing construction, engine power, and aerodynamic theory were conceived first. Lawsuits became common because so many wanted the fortune and notoriety that came with being first. Many aviators were trying to claim recognition in national air races, aviation meets, and aeronautical-related events. The desperate nature of the aviation world at the time may have caused the air pioneer to do some uncommon things. Some who lived in Gilmore's day said that he was secretive about his experiments, that he would purposely leave out parts of his planes' designs. Some say that at times he neglected to include vital parts of engines he used when trying to get a patent for fear that someone else would steal his ideas. At times, he avoided the press. Others say that he didn't understand the business world, and people were sometimes confused about his ideas. The authorities at the patent office would often discredit ideas he submitted because of his unconventional writing style. Sometimes he would create designs but wouldn't try to market the ideas or do anything with them. All of this challenged his credibility within the aviation community.

Living in the newly developed west where the population was smaller may have also greatly affected his success. Investors may not have known about him. The eastern cities were more industrialized, and aviators there had easier access to machines.

Still others believe that his plane designs weren't sufficient. The materials and engines he used weren't strong enough to make a plane fly in a level position as we see planes fly today. Of course, we now know that the engines Lyman was using were inadequate. The steam engines of his day too—with their boilers, furnaces, and other required essentials—were heavy. The early motors produced too little power for the weight of the planes.

The inventor and engineer always thought that not enough money was spent on his planes. People who invested in his ventures fell through with their promises or just couldn't come up with enough capital so the planes could be built correctly. Even then, planes were expensive to build. As always, finances and poor luck seemed to play a big part in the success or failure of his endeavors.

Lyman Gilmore Jr. believed that inventions that changed how man lived from day to day "were conceived by inspired visionary geniuses like him." Unfortunately, he was filled with ideas and details of how to make inventions but was never able to take credit for his genius. He was never appropriately recognized for his contributions because the events of his life are sketchy and unrecorded. There is no mention of his name in most history books. His face doesn't adorn a stamp or coin. However, next time you visit an airport or look high into the sky to see a passenger jetliner, you can think about the humble beginnings of all this on Lyman's field and in his workshop.

Chapter Eight

Lyman's Awards and Inventions

Lyman Gilmore Jr. was known as a Guggenheim scholar. A payment from the Daniel Guggenheim Fund, in recognition of his contribution to powered flight, was awarded to him for coming up with the know-how to build an airplane wing with superior lift. The fund also reflected the scientific community's respect for the man's achievements by giving him a diploma. This honored his efforts in gaining attention to aviation in the western cities and states and trying to get other flying fields established. Sometime before 1930, Lyman's airport was recognized by the fund for the promotion of aviation. He had placed a wind sock atop a tall pole using it as a weather instrument to indicate wind direction. This, along with other characteristics of an airport, appeared to make the it identifiable from the air. Indications that the Lyman Gilmore Field was named as an airport, at least until 1949, are documented by a United States geological survey map. The field was also home to a local flight school until 1947. Between 1954 and 1957, an area on the other side of town became home to the county airport, which remains operating today.

Lyman Gilmore Jr. invented many other things. Many of his inventions were never patented. However, there is evidence of patents he received between 1945 and 1950 for a rotary snowplow used to clear railroad tracks. This type of snowplow is used even today to clear snow from the busy freeways and highways during heavy snowfalls. A carbide lighting system he installed in homes, experimentation with solar heat and power, and developing a way to economize the gasoline engine were ideas patented during this time.

He drew designs for a submarine chaser in 1916. In addition, he gave the United States government advice about weapon systems from 1941 to 1944 during World War II. In fact, one man attested to seeing a vividly detailed description of World War II, its aftermath, and reconstruction by Lyman Gilmore Jr. in a journal that was shown to him by Gilmore himself in 1919.

The air pioneer helped to build the 160-foot cantilever bridge, making way for the local railroad system, called the Nevada County Narrow Gauge Railroad, to operate. Manuscripts have been found of a few science-fiction stories he wrote. Other writings were found that talked about converting arid desert regions in the Middle Eastern countries into a land of agriculture.

Drawings revealing designs of a "radial eight" or eight-piston engine, his small monoplane, large monoplane, and blueprints of his airfield remain. The eight-cylinder radial motor he designed used diesel fuel and had three moving parts: crankshaft, piston, and connecting rods. All valves, cams, and spark plugs were eliminated. He declared that it would run as long as there was fuel or one of the vital parts didn't break. This motor was designed before the Curtiss 0 x 5 motor was marketed.

Among other inventions he reportedly made were designs of a three hundred-foot long merchant marine submarine, war machines including an antiaircraft cannon, landing barges used during World War II, and a shaft-boring machine that could cut through shale and bedrock. None of these ideas were ever patented.

According to a family manuscript, Lyman designed a self-operating pump that could draw water from the mines. Finally, one other invention credited to the aeronautical engineer is a plane with motor that takes off from and lands safely on a small area such as a flat roof, similar to our modern-day helicopter.

A film of Lyman Gilmore Jr. working in his hangar with his brother Charles still exists today. The movie short shows the two working alongside the big eight-passenger cabin monoplane and thumbing through a journal of Lyman's drawings and designs. The crumpled remains of the small monoplane lay in the background. This film was made in 1931 by a newspaper cartoonist named John Hix. The movie short was made by Scientific Films Incorporated.

A concrete bench and historic plaque describing how Chinese people built the rails sits at Promontory Point in Colfax. This point sits atop a ridge across from the tip of Cape Horn.

The Gilmore Airship Company became the Gilmore Airplane Company and raised up to $500,000 for commercial aviation and manufacturing during its time.

After Lyman Gilmore's death, stock certificates from the Gilmore Airship Company were sold as souvenirs or collector's items for 25¢ cents each. The last certificate was sold in the year 2000.

The Gilmore Airfield is known for being the first commercial airfield in the United States. Some people believe that the field, planes, and hangars formed America's first commercial airport. It has also been suggested that the airport was the oldest in existence.

Conclusion

Lyman Gilmore Jr.'s last request was that his estate be used "to promote the knowledge and science of mechanical engineering." This request was partially met in an interesting way.

In the early 1960s, my father became the school superintendent of the Grass Valley School District. The city of Grass Valley badly needed a new junior high school to accommodate future generations of children. In 1965, a school bond was passed in the city's general election.

My father and the city school board then worked to buy the Gilmore Field from the Cooley Butler estates. Mr. Butler lived in the Los Angeles area and owned different properties at the time.

On November 2, 1968, a dedication ceremony was held to honor the completion of the school that was named the Lyman Gilmore School.

Aside from being a point of historical interest, the school continues to operate as a middle school even today. In recent years, other buildings have also been built on the property that was once the Gilmore Field. A grassy ball field is all that is left of the original flying field, and the pole that held the old wind sock remains standing now, adorning a modern wind sock. A historical plaque is nearby.

To this day, Lyman Gilmore Jr. remains a part of local folklore. Even so, his life and contributions remain very real and remind us that Mr. Gilmore was among the pioneers of aviation who pushed its progress leading toward the convenience of flight in our modern world.

*　　*　　*

If still standing, the Lyman Gilmore Field would be one hundred years old in the year 2007.

Author's Notes

There are many conflicting dates and facts about Lyman Gilmore Jr. and his circumstances. Following are just a few of the many inconsistencies of this poorly documented case, which make the search for the truth about the airfield a difficult one.

*　　*　　*

The date for Lyman Gilmore Jr.'s birth year as 1876 was chosen from information within a family manuscript and on his gravestone at the Pine Grove Cemetery in Nevada City, California. Many articles written about him state that his birth year was 1874.

Some writings state that Mr. Gilmore was born in Mokelumne Hill, California. Other writings say that his birthplace was in one of two places in the Washington Territory, Sightly in Cowlitz County, and Beaver Creek in Thurston County.

An old newspaper article stated that Lyman Gilmore Sr. travelled across the plains of America to settle in California. It has also been written that Lyman Gilmore Sr. travelled from the East Coast on ship around the cape of South America to settle in California.

Some accounts say Lyman first experimented in Castle Rock, Washington. Other accounts say he was in Oregon.

There have been differences of opinion about the location of the hangar built to house the birdlike passenger monoplane. Most articles written about the story point to Gilmore Field being home to the hangar. However, there has also been mention of the hangar being built in Red Bluff, California. Contradictory information points to the large plane being destroyed by fire in 1907 or 1935.

One story has been told about Lyman Gilmore Jr. piloting a plane and racing a Curtiss engineer to San Francisco in 1918. Gilmore's monoplane, which carried three passengers, beat the Curtiss plane by one-half hour. Another story tells of Lyman flying to different cities along the West Coast. However, a local newspaper article written in 1925 states that Lyman Gilmore piloted a regular plane for the first time in 1925.

One local recollection states that Lyman Gilmore Jr. and his brother Charles were twins who were born in the Mokelumne Hill area.

The story here, as well as in other accounts, relays that the building of Lyman Gilmore Jr.'s monoplanes took place around 1907 and 1908. However, there are other claims that one or both of these planes was already built when the airfield opened. One writing states that the small monoplane was built between 1909 and 1911. One writing speaks of Lyman Gilmore Jr. building monoplane-like planes as early as 1898.

Lyman had different companies, and at times, the names changed.

Note: This book was written to create interest in Lyman Gilmore Jr. and does not necessarily reflect all the facts in this case.

Special Thanks

California State Library—Sacramento, CA
Colfax Historical Society
Colfax Record Newspaper
Doris Foley Library—Nevada City, CA
Hillard Aviation Museum, Northern California
Illustrators—Chris Marinan and Bill Bruce
Living citizens who have met Lyman Gilmore Jr.
Searles Library
Nevada City, CA
U.S. Census
Washington State Library

Made in the USA
San Bernardino, CA
06 March 2013